CAUTION: Deadline Ahead

A comedy (book!) about procrastination

CRISTINA LARK

ISBN paperback: 978-1-9161621-0-5
ISBN ebook: 978-1-9161621-1-2

"You have goals, you have plans, you have a brilliant future ahead. But you also have Candy Crush, Facebook, and 1,035 unread emails that you decided now is a good time to sort. Welcome to Cristina's brain, an entity of its own, with its own will, who's convinced that the concept of time is an illusion and that it's suddenly a great moment to read about it online."

Are you tired of leading a boring life with no thrill?

Do you long for that kick of adrenaline that keeps you on edge and makes you feel alive?

Look no further!

Join millions of humans in this tried and tested practice that's guaranteed to make you panic in the most avoidable situations, and rush like there's no tomorrow, because if you miss the deadline... there may not be.

PROCRASTIN-8

With PROCRASTIN-8, no task with a deadline will go by without the exciting feeling that in the end you'll pull it off. In an epic move. Assisted by your favourite superhero sidekick:

God!
(who always shows up to save your ass)

Important paper to deliver at uni? Why waste your precious time researching like a loser and putting all that effort into writing coherent sentences, when you can power-through a night-before all-nighter and deliver half-assed work that's going to do the job anyway?

Tax return to fill? Why waste your precious month among invoices and receipts, when you can power-through a last-minute all-nighter and deliver numbers that at least won't get you in jail?

Don't waste any more time and get on board right now. Because... if you practice procrastination... that's the only thing you're going to be able to start right now anyway.

PROCRASTIN-8: a better tomorrow for you.

Side effects include: non-completion of any personal project without a deadline, overall underachievement, mediocrity, and chronic self-loathing.

****

I'm not too sure when or where, but I must have taken this drug at some point in my childhood. I'm a chronic procrastinator.

Don't get me wrong. I'm great at completing mechanical tasks with clear beginning, middle, end and a deadline. With clear pre-organised information that is readily available to simply input, and with an outcome that offers zero risk or confrontation. None of which is characteristic of any entrepreneurial venture, or artistic project.

It would be a sweet life for me. If I wasn't an artist and an entrepreneur.

I find it so chic, entrepreneurs who get shit done in a timely manner. People who are always on-the-go, crossing items off their to-do list, in an app that they know how to use, and finding time to have quality fun afterwards, always advancing their careers, prestige and financial situation.

But I can't have this, because I suffer from a severe psychological disorder. It's called "The Blank Canvas Syndrome". It's a serious condition that you develop, ok? Because when you have one clear task, the only hurdle you have to overcome is breaking the inertia and start. But when you have a blank canvas, the freedom of managing your own time and starting anything from sheer scratch, and you have lots of ideas for projects, then a mysterious blocking starts occurring: *Which am I going to start with? Where do I start? How do I even start? Do I even need to start this one now? Ok, let me just mop the floor first to clear my head, and then I'll get cracking with it. You know what's more important? Making the money I'm making right now, with this dull, dead-end source of income. Priorities, right?* When you realise, weeks, months, years have passed, and you haven't even managed to start working on that project you really wanted to do.

And this is how I ended up taking 8 years to finally write and tour my first ever one-woman show, from the moment I first learned that it was a possibility for me, a non-celebrity actor, to simply write and tour a show (you don't have to be hired or receive millions in government grants) to the moment I went up on stage for the premiere.

The show, not ironically, is called **"CAUTION: Deadline Ahead - A comedy about procrastination"**, and I've toured it for a year now.

The writing process, however, went a bit like this:

10

Yes. And next thing I know, 2 more years will have passed, and everything will still be in my hard drive. So this is the right moment to do it. I'm inspired, I'm in flow, I'm in the zone. I'm sure it's gonna be a quick job.

3 Months Later...

Time-lapse Fairy

* If you're a music nerd and you want to know the exact melody, you can find it on page 118. Yes, I made a score. Yes, one month AFTER the LAST performance. Yes, I was running away from a more important (and more boring) task.

I'm actually great at starting things and never finishing them.

It's so exciting, starting things... Because it's all about the idea. You picture yourself in the future, having accomplished those amazing deeds... and completely disregard all the work that it entails. You only see the results.

For instance, I always wanted to *have done* a solo comedy show, in the past. But who would have thought that to do a show, you need to actually WRITE it? And you don't just sit and start typing like you've been possessed by the Creativity Fairy, no, no no. Who would have thought that you'll be staring at a blank screen for ages? And that your screen is so dirty? And that there's so much shit stuck in between the keys of your keyboard?

This part is going to get a bit intense, so I recommend we play a drinking game. One of those "never-have-I-ever" drinking games, so you drink every time you have never done what I say. If it's too early for booze, just grab a hot beverage, or some water. Here we go:

Who in here has never taken a business card, or a folded post-it, and started to carve out that little mass of dust, hair and crumbs that gathers in between the keys of a keyboard? Especially the older keyboard models, where the gap is bigger. There's something deliciously satisfactory about that. Double points if you've ever found a fingernail. I have found my share of fingernails on computer keyboards. Mainly in the office. And I don't clip my nails in the office. So if I find clipped nails, they're clearly someone else's. Third party. Maybe from an older employee, from God knows how long ago, and it just puzzles me and fills me with questions and-

Is it just me?

Please tell me it's not just me.

Anyway, moving on...

Who would have thought that the more you have to think, the more you are going to be strangely, magnetically, attracted to your fridge?

Imagine you're working on something really important or difficult, that requires thought. Not just something mechanical, but something that involves high stakes, that involves you *creating* something.

This is what happens:

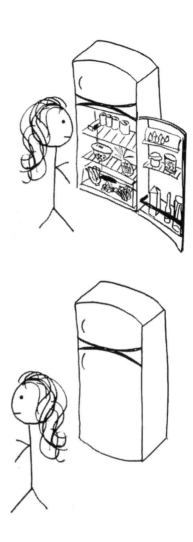

5 minutes later...

You still have the same stumbling block. Or maybe another stumbling block.

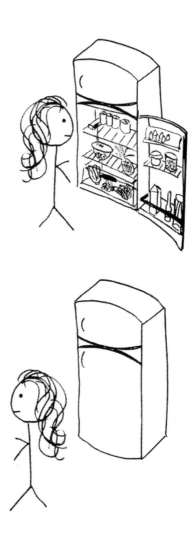

Most of the times we don't even eat anything!

We're like teleguided hypnotized zombies.

Drink if you've never opened your fridge to think.

Drink if you've never stopped whatever you were doing, with the urge of googling something random.

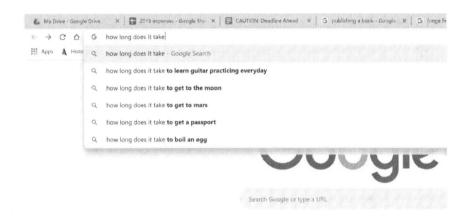

Yes, I always wanted to *have done* a comedy show and then *have written* a book about it, and I'd say I've made good progress so far. With that infomercial that I wrote at the beginning, and that little song that I started to compose, I have achieved what, in my books, is a very intensive 3-minute session of hard work. I totally deserve a break! It's well earned, well deserved!

So, let's keep playing the drinking game.

Who in here has never procrastinated? About anything?

If you're drinking now, I'm gonna call bullshit.

Because everyone thinks about *others* procrastinating as them being lazy, unorganized, or even coward (you've heard it I'm sure, especially from those friends of yours into "mindset work": "Oh, this is fear of failure! / fear of success!"). But it's not that simple.

I, for instance, procrastinate on stuff that would be really fulfilling, really pleasurable, really useful to move me forward with my life. Because I found out that I suffer from a severe psychological disorder. It's called...

The Brussel Sprout Syndrome.

It's a serious condition that you develop, ok? And I blame my mum for that: because when I was a kid, I knew exactly what I wanted, I had it right in front of me, I was going for it. And then, my mother would say: "you're not eating this chocolate lava cake until you finish your Brussel sprouts".

And so it began. Since my childhood, I've been eating the Brussel sprouts of life, like I'm yet to *earn* the chocolate lava cake of life. The chocolate lava cake never comes. It's always "for later", for after I've stomached something bitter and horrible, and that's supposed to be "what's good for me".

No, you don't. There's no scientific correlation whatsoever of cause and effect. But we're conditioned to think there is. We're conditioned to think that pleasure is only a reward. But now that we're all adults, unsupervised by our parents, and probably into much more hardcore drugs, try eating a spoonful of dessert before your meal.

[drum roll]

Nothing happens.

Or maybe I'm guaranteed to go to hell as soon as I die, who knows what's on tap for me?

But come on, let's be fair here. I can't just blame my mum for everything that ever goes wrong in my life. Let's be mature, let's be adults. It's not just my mum's fault.

I blame my dad as well.

Just for genetics. My dad was born in Barcelona, and you know how some cities in the world have an iconic monument that symbolizes them internationally? Like Sydney has the Opera, Rio has the Christ, Paris has the Eiffel Tower... Barcelona's symbol is a cathedral that's been under construction since 1882. The guy who started building it died before he could finish. And then others took over, and the job is still going! And you know what they said, in 2011? That it might be ready possibly by 2028!

Now, can you imagine this being an acceptable, plausible excuse for you to use in your personal or professional life?

What the fuck, right?

This is the Barcelona cathedral. The Sagrada Familia, if you want to pay to see it.

And this is kind of what's in my blood, I guess. Starting things and never finishing them. If I never had a deadline, I don't think I'd ever finish ANYTHING. Not that having deadlines makes me a better functioning human. Because this goes way back: in school, if a teacher said "you have 97 years to deliver your essay", I'd pretty much start working on it 96 years, 11 months and 2 weeks later.

In school, I would do all my homework the night before it was due. Until I realized I could do it through the night! And I did that! Until I realized I could start early in the morning on the day the task was due! And why finish at home, when you have all those spare minutes on the school bus to finish throwing glitter on your little science project?

And I clearly remember that epic day when the teacher said: "Cristina, answer to question number 14!", so I stood up, read the question... ignored those blank lines underneath it where the written answer was supposed to be... and I started speaking as if I was reading an articulate paragraph. All my classmates went looking at my notebook, looking at me, looking at my notebook, looking at me. Astonished.

Even all my bullies, for that one second, were like: "Respect."

*yes, this is the Hunger Games salute.

I started priding myself in school years for being able to always pull it off in the end. So that became "my thing". "That's how I roll".

And roll I did... through adulthood... Running, dishevelled, shoes in hands, the airplane gates closing in before me like in an Indiana Jones' movie, my boarding pass cut in half... but I was in! I had made it! Again! The plane taking off, I was soaring through the sky... whilst every other passenger onboard was looking at me like that angry mob of Cairo villagers in an Indiana Jones' movie.

You see, believing you can always pull it off in the end makes procrastinators great at being always late as well. There is a correlation.

Now, let's debunk some myths here.

Myth number 1: Being always late is a matter of lack of respect for others

No. Us, chronically late procrastinators have a pathological optimism, and live in denial about how time works.

For instance. Say I need to meet someone at a coffee shop at 3pm.

This is what happens in my mind. This is how I firmly believe things will play out.

And this - is what actually happens:

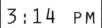

3:14 PM

Hi! Hey! Sorry! OMG, the train was delayed, and the traffic was crazy, and I couldn't find my keys when I was leaving, and- I'm so sorry, how long were you waiting? OMG, sorry!

2:59 PM

Come on, train, FASTER! Come on, little blue dot on Google Maps! Faster! FASTER!

2:10 PM

Hmm... I guess it's ok if I leave at quarter past. Trains are fast, reliable, and never experience unexpected delays. Plus, that thing I've been trying to do all morning, I'm finally so focused to do it now. I'm sure I can wrap this up in 5 min.

I have issues.

Which brings me to:

Myth number 2: Procrastination happens due to lack of willpower.

Everybody has a little shoulder devil, and a little shoulder angel, and everybody knows that you should listen to the angel.

Like the devil will say:

And the angel will say:

That makes a lot of sense. If your shoulder angel's not an asshole like mine.

66

Yes. Willpower is the least of my concerns. The thing is that us procrastinators love keeping ourselves busy with eternal preparation, as an excuse to forever put off the stuff that really matters. Because not only the stuff that really matters is the chocolate lava cake, but it also involves very high stakes. And it's like, while we don't act, we live in that sweet limbo of potential glory, that only hasn't come to be yet because we haven't triggered anything yet.

Are we a failure? Are we a success?

Who knows? While we don't try, we can be both. That's what I call the Schrodinger's Cat state of success.

A bit of a parenthesis: the Schrodinger's Cat state of success can apply to everything, even relationships. A male friend of mine once told me that he procrastinates on texting girls. He says *"While I don't text that girl I matched and I fancy, I've both been rejected and scored. But as of now, the situation status is "She gave me her number". And who, in their right frame of mind, would ever want to ruin this by taking action and seeing what actually happens?"*

But when I say "we don't act", it's not that we're spending all the afternoon blankly staring at the ceiling. We are doing *something*. The problem is that what we are doing is detrimental both to just completing our work already AND to our quality leisure time. Because you know, just as well as I do, that procrastination activities go way beyond the typical "cleaning your whole kitchen before starting to work" - although I must admit that this *is* the perfect time to totally un-goo the detergent bottle cap on your sink - they go way beyond the TO-DO LIST OF DOOM - the classic "before starting to work on this project, I need to sort the files on my external hard drive and my Google Drive, which also means reading all the docs there to see what they are about and see which ones I can delete *(at which point you'll see all the parked ideas that you once started working on and muse for some extra 20 minutes in a spiral of hopelessness and anxiety)*, and before that I need to update all the spreadsheets that I found in the process. Where was my box of receipts?".

And procrastination activities are totally different than, like some people who don't know what procrastination means would believe, "just thinking about it". When I did this show in festivals, I'd flyer people, saying this is a show about procrastination, and some older men who think they are hilarious and super original, would say, *"I'll think about it. Ha-ha. See what I did there? Eh? Eh? I'm procrastinating. He-he".* No, Jeff. This would be indecision. Procrastination is not just musing about whether or not to do something.

And since we're talking about what procrastination is not (yes, this will be a bit of a digression), let's make clear that there are some fake procrastinators out there. They're those people who say *"I totally watched 2 episodes of a series yesterday on Netflix instead of just one, I'm such a procrastinator... but hey, you need to enjoy life as well! You'll work better afterwards!"*

If you're methodically allocating 2 hours of your day for leisure instead of one, as a reward for your hard work, and after this extra hour you manage to work more productively, you're not a real procrastinator, sorry.

Some so-called procrastinators just don't know how real the struggle can be. They're cute. And highly enviable. Some others try to pass as procrastinators in the most obnoxious way (cue to real dialogue I had):

Let's take a closer look at this real dialogue that I had with someone on Facebook, during my research phase for writing the show, with a dude who offered to explain how he procrastinates:

Dear dude,

1) Allocating time to go to the gym, buy groceries or shower is not procrastination. It's basic hygiene, and all it indicates is that your mum doesn't go grocery shopping for you (well done!). People who are not "their own bosses" hopefully also find time to shower and buy food. They also need to do all these things.

2) "Whatever I'd like to do" is only an acceptable answer if you're under 5. Even children have responsibilities. You can't just skip a meeting with a client, refrain from processing your invoices, or ignore questions from your team just because "you're your own boss". Please tell me the name of your consulting agency so I never hire your services.

3) I'm glad this conversation is more rewarding to you than... wait, *frying some eggs and then taking a shower?* I thought we were talking about what you were supposed to be doing instead of being on Facebook having this conversation, since you said you "procrastinate" to distance yourself from a problem you can't solve. If "frying eggs" and "showering" fall under "problems you can't solve", I'd go ahead and guess you do live with your mum, after all.

4) You're going to launch a whole "procrastination course" based on this conversation? What is it going to teach? "How to spend your precious time self-indulging and oozing toxic masculinity on the internet?" "Module One - Showcasing your poor business management skills to strangers: it's more rewarding than frying some eggs?"

Having leisure in unconventional hours is not procrastination. No one procrastinates on purpose, in an allocated slot on their daily calendar. If you say "I'm going to procrastinate for just 2 hours and watch this movie instead of working", and you KNOW that in 2 exact hours you'll be doing your work... and you do it... sorry mate, you have no idea what the struggle is.

(end of digression, and look, there's a hook!)

Procrastination activities are not any of the above. The problem is that these activities are generally completely pointless work, that often takes a lot of time, or it's work that people in the right frame of mind would just look and say "just ditch it forever and don't waste any other second of your life on this!

For instance, whilst trying to make this show into a book, I got so caught up with "perfecting" the illustrations, that I spent 3 whole weeks on photoshop just manually retouching every individual pixel from the scanned hand drawings, and 3 more weeks doing a LOT of rework: first I made illustrations with no text, then I added the text and dialogue balloons to each image (worked better for Google Docs), then erased all of them and recreated the balloons on the document (worked better for Word), then replaced all of them again with the ones that had text (worked better for Kindle), etc. Any functional person would have finished in a week, put in on sale already, and moved on to a more important project.

Gladly (or not), I'm not alone. I hang out in cesspools of chronic procrastinators: Facebook groups for entrepreneurs. With their self-proclaimed coaching gurus, self-proclaimed business owners, where everybody is a self-proclaimed CEO of something. You guys, you have no idea how many unemployed people there are out there. If someone says "I'm a CEO", it generally means "I'm unemployed, I have a lot of time in my hands and I have no actual deadline". And most of these people are examples that perfectly illustrate the time-consuming pointlessness of procrastination activities. Because the first thing you need to have in place in order to call yourself a CEO, a business owner, is an income. It's a constant influx of paying clients. But you ask any neo-entrepreneur in the group, and they will say they "first need to work on their website".

Let's examine that. You start DYIing your website, because it's easier to do it yourself, plus it's free, and only a dork would pay anyone, because nowadays ALL THE ANSWERS CAN BE FOUND ON THE INTERNET. You start, believing it's going to be a 30-minute job. How hard can it be? Then you realise it's a bit more complicated than you originally thought. There's this form that needs a codec that needs customising, which needs a bit of googling. So you keep googling, and googling, and googling for the next stumbling block, and next thing you know 3 weeks have passed and you may or may not have registered for module 5 of Java Script on Codecademy. Now apparently you're studying web development. You're a web development student. You got completely off track.

But you firmly believe that you're working, that you're busy. After all, you haven't showered in 3 days, you're still in your pyjamas, you have no groceries left, you're surviving on milk and cereal! You're hustling, you tell yourself. You're not being productive, and you're not having fun either. You're only doing a lot of random stuff that's not taking you anywhere. And I don't know why! I don't know why we do this.

What I do know is how to get away from this. How our brain tries to get us out of this pickle. (Pickle Rick!)

You obviously know, as a responsible adult, that you can't just go and have fun. Having fun, now, would be completely unearned, and you'd be filled with guilt, anxiety and self-hatred.

You need to concentrate, but your brain tries to help you escape. So your brain makes you start tapping random icons on your phone, or opening random tabs on your computer.

You're still at your desk, you're still in front of your computer, and you have rightfully turned down an invitation to watch a movie or go out... "I've got WORK to do!", you proudly say. But people came BACK from the fun date, and you realise 2 hours and 40 minutes have passed and you're just scrolling through your social media feed. Or you're now looking at all the 600 Facebook vacation photos of that previous university classmate who wasn't even a friend. You've decided to visit, for the first time, Lady Gaga's Instagram. You've decided to browse the hashtag #PickleRick, because you remembered it's a thing.

There's one exception to "not doing actual fun stuff" that we procrastinators make, and it's playing games on our phone. Don't get me wrong, this is still totally unearned fun, and it still fills us with guilt, anxiety and self-hatred. But a fascinating weird phenomenon happens: at the same time that you're self-loathing for not doing anything else that would be more productive, it also provides you with a happy place of denial, cushioned exclusively with positive reinforcement. You generally see this cute little panda (or whatever cute little character), with these cute little eyes, and all the words that come out of the screen are positive: Awesome! Fantastic! Brilliant! Well done! Chic! Powerful!

Also, these games give you the illusion that it's going to be quick - it's not like you're committing to playing a proper videogame, which you'd only do in your actual leisure time - and at the same time they give you the illusion that you are achieving something. But there's no end! They have infinite levels! And the extra tasks! Oh, the extra tasks! The rankings and competitions! If nothing else will hook you, they will! You'll miss the times you'd SET ALARM CLOCKS in the middle of the night to harvest your crops on Farmville before they withered (which I never did, ok?).

So I wonder if there were simpler times in life. Times where people just got shit done. Because they didn't have the option of leaving it for tomorrow, they couldn't afford to procrastinate. It was either win, or die trying. What would have happened, to us, humans, as a species, if our ancestors had procrastinated in pressing times? What would have happened if the bravest people in human history had procrastinated? Actually, wait a minute. We descend from these people. We have their genes. And according to Darwin, we are the natural selection. If we're here today, it's because the procrastinators of the past had the fittest genes. So maybe the story that we learned from history lessons and Disney movies is not exactly how it happened. THIS is what's more likely to have happened among our ancestors:

Look at their king with all those insane gangsta chains around his chest! Whoa! Which whey protein is he on?

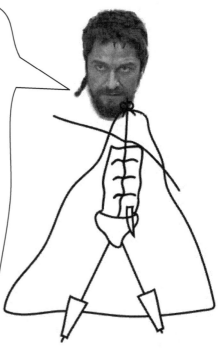

Plus, who's gonna respect a group of only 300 people nowadays? It's not influencing enough. Maybe we just stay here taking pictures of ourselves until we reach 10k FOLLOWERS!... That would impose some more respect, yeah? Give us more credibility? Maybe even land us a decent brand deal. Can't really go out there and be seen wearing this crap. What the f*ck, guys, who had the genius idea to say that all we needed to pack for this battle was underwear, knee-high boots and capes? Honestly!

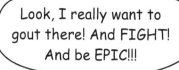

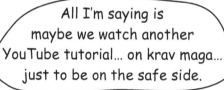
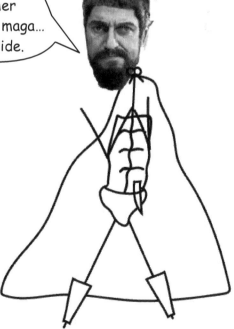

Oh! Oh! Hahaha!
That reminds me of that video – you must have seen it, it went viral – with this guy trying some krav maga moves, wearing a pink bunny onesie, whilst talking to some girls on Chatroulette. Haha, that's so classic, have you guys seen it? No? Can we just watch it real quick so you can see it? It's so funny, you have to! Real quick!

No? We have no time?

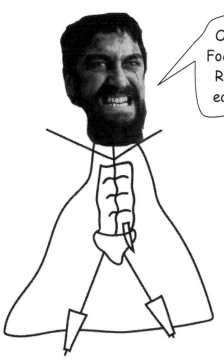

Ok! No more distractions! Focus we must! SPARTANS!! Ready your breakfast and eat hearty. For tonight we dine IN HELL!

Or maybe tomorrow...? How far are they? I'd say 2 more days of walking, at least. I reckon there's time to get some pizza, have some drinks... let's play some Fortnite!

Ok. It didn't happen this way. Maybe we don't descend from the bravest people in human history after all, and having the fittest genes meant the ability our ancestors had to just tag along with those who did pull the weight in ancient times. Maybe as a group, as a tribe, procrastinators didn't really have to meet deadlines alone, so their genes ended up making it in the gene pool all the way to the present just by hanging around.

Or maybe this is what would have happened if the people from the past, brave or not, had all these distractions that we have available nowadays. They would eventually have gone to battle last minute, rushing, panicking, but not without a lot of slacking in the preceding days.

Deadlines make us procrastinators rush and panic, that's no #mindblow information. But we only rush and panic when we HAVE a deadline hot on our heels. We postpone the task till it's almost too late, but we do it, regardless of the quality of the results. The biggest problem for us procrastinators is when there's absolutely no external deadline for the stuff we want to do. These are generally artistic or entrepreneurial ventures. These are generally things that depend on us and us alone, that society is in no way pushing us to do. Like learning a musical instrument, learning a foreign language, learning photography... or starting a side hustle, that passion project... or even exercising. You're not going to go to jail for not doing these things. You're not going to lose your job. You're not going to die. You're not going to be publicly embarrassed. Your doctor may suggest that you exercise, you may wish you were in better shape, but the truth is, there's no rush outside of your own determination. You may want to open this can of worms and argue that "society constantly wants me to lose weight", but that's less and less the case. See, for instance, an archive of my aunt Amelia's New Year resolution lists through the years (ah, New Year resolution lists... the foretold obituary of our plans and goals...):

3 years ago: "I want to drop 5 kg"

2 years ago: "I want to drop 10kg"

Last year: "I want to drop 15kg"

This year: "I WANT TO FIGHT THE OPPRESSIVE BEAUTY STANDARDS THAT SOCIETY IMPOSES ON US! #BodyPositivity!!!"

See? When there are no external deadlines, we can keep procrastinating forever. Add that to the new set of distractions that technology provided, and you'll have a new breed of non-achievers who live in complete denial about their situation:

I'm actually not. I'm only here in group therapy because my mum makes me. I just have multiple interests that don't fit in the traditional schooling system, that's totally different. But my mum says I have never accomplished anything in life.

Wait until she sees the level I am on Candy Crush.

You know how hard Candy Crush can get? It's hard, man. There are levels that take days, even weeks to pass. And you have to keep coming back, over and over, and trying, and trying, and trying... If that's not determination, I honestly don't know what is.

And it requires a whole set of skills, as well. Creativity. Thinking outside the box. Hacking the system. For instance... when you run out of lives, you can go back to your phone's settings, date and time, and advance the clock 3 hours or more. This way, all your 5 lives will be restored! Did you know that? Who knew this? This woman here is looking at me thinking "OMG, what a genius idea!" You're welcome. You can do that. Or, if you're like me, you can download a bunch of other games that you can play in a little circuit of games, to wait for the lives to be restored naturally. That's what? Process optimization, system implementation... That's so perfect.

Oh! Perfection, that's it! People say that procrastinators are actually perfectionists. Maybe that's why my mum thinks I'm a procrastinator, because I _am_ a perfectionist! When I play Angry Birds – you guys remember, Angry Birds? Is it still a thing? I love it - if the first bird slingshot is just meh, I need to start again! 'Cause it needs to be perfect! I need to make the biggest impact, using the least amount of resources, in the most logistically optimised route... There's a lot of business skills there.

Speaking of business, I'm thinking of starting one. A YouTube channel. And since I'm not a procrastinator, as soon as I had the idea, I went straight to my computer and I googled "how to start a YouTube channel". On google. On the internet. Which means... 3 hours later I was reading my tenth blog post!

Have you realized how all blogs posts are evil? They have those evil links in the middle of the text to other interesting articles that you kinda need to read as well to complement the information. They're like those Russian dolls, with infinite dolls! And then you keep clicking to read the next. You keep clicking and opening, and clicking and opening, and clicking and opening...

Whoah! That's exhausting! Can we play a drinking game? Just to relax?

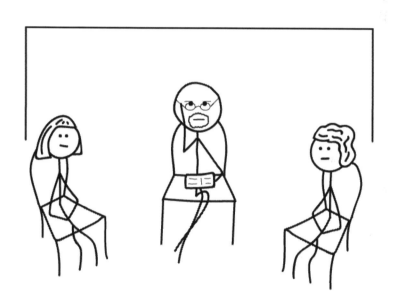

No? It's not allowed? That's not the AA, you know? Whatever. I'm gonna do it anyway! Here I go!

Who in here has never gotten to that stage in your browser when you see infinite microscopic little tabs that you can't possibly read that day? Who has never closed their laptop without turning it off, so you can pick up the morning after from where you stopped? Who has never had a looong list of bookmarked links that you're "saving for later", but they've been sitting there for weeks, for months, for YEARS!!!??? Who in here is a digital HOARDER? Like pictures on your phone!!! You have 4,000 pictures on your phone, clogging the memory, you can't do anything, not even send a WhatsApp message, and all the pictures are shit, BUT YOU CAN'T SEEM TO DELETE ANY???

Who in here is an email hoarder???

I remember those dark days, when I would decide to clean my inbox... I'd decide this was the most appropriate thing to do to put me "in the right frame of mind to start applying for jobs"... 3 whole days would pass, I'd be there non-showered, wearing the same pyjamas, surviving on milk and cereal, before I realized what the f*ck I was doing. I'd think it would be "a quick job", sorting my unread emails...
I HAD 1,563 OF THEM!!!

But no more! I came up now with a fantastic method to sort all the emails in your inbox! Do you want to know what it is? I'll teach you, pay attention: you go to the very first email, you know, click as many times as you have to on the arrow that says "emails 1-50 of 9,896,564", go to the first one, open it, read it, take a very good look at it, then close your eyes, and ask yourself: "Is this email sparking joy?"

I came up with it myself. You can thank me.

No, of course that doesn't work! Because by the time you're on email number six, 400 new emails just poured in! They never stop coming!! I tried! I tried the diligent way! I had to open them, read them, click on the link, read the article... and you know what I found out? By email 237, that was, like, from June 2015 or something?

I found out that most of those emails that you've been saving for ages... they contain links... that lead nowhere...! They don't exist! 404 - page not found!

Which means... that the article writer, the blog owner, the course creator... have moved on with their lives... BUT I HAVEN'T! I'M STILL THERE!!! Hanging out in a ghost town... clinging to the memory of something that is no more... That was too much for me...

So I decided to go where the people are...

YouTube.

Now, I know what you're thinking, ok? "D'uh, that's the part when she talks about those YouTube spirals of doom, you know, those that start with innocent videos, like "how to poach an egg", and end with "top 5 weirdest sightings that prove mermaids are real".

But no, ok? I'm not going to talk about that. I never go on a YouTube spiral of random videos. Everything I watch is totally on purpose, it's research. So that's why I consciously watched... all the videos on why Harry Potter books are better than the movies. And videos on why Harry Potter movies are better than the books. And videos analyzing the differences between both. And videos with theories that say that Dumbledore is actually gay!

And then, when I watched all of them –
yes, I've watched ALL of them - I went on Facebook, on Reddit.

I wanted to see what other people's opinion was. I wanted to join the conversation. So I started reading the comments... I started commenting as well... I started getting on fights with random strangers over stuff that I totally don't care about... and next thing I know... I WAS TALKING ABOUT HITLER!!!

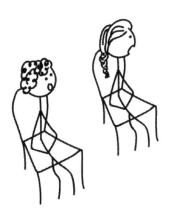

But then, on my newsfeed, I saw a link to this video and the following caption: "3 little ducklings are crossing the road... You'll never know what happens next"! ... well, not if I don't click and watch the whole thing, I won't. So I clicked. And I watched.

These posts always get me: "13 potatoes that totally look like Channing Tatum, number 7 will BLOW YOUR MIND!"..., "Watch this video! It will restore your faith in HUMANITY!"... "Click on this link. It will CHANGE. YOUR. LIFE!"... I clearly need my life to change. I mean, look at me! Plus, every time I take that BuzzFeed quiz "Which Star Wars Characters Are You?", I get JAR JAR BINKS!!! I tried over and over again, and I always get the same result! So I took another test! I took "Which city in the world are you?"... and I got Milton Keynes. There isn't even a Milton Keynes option, I'm sure. But I get it. So I clearly need a life-changing spell, to change my life for the better, so I click away, and I watch away... But my mind remains unblown, I still have no faith in humanity, and my life hasn't changed. I'm starting to think these posts overpromise, a bit? Because how many times can a single life TOTALLY change? And what kind of life changes by whatever is in those links?

96

All those deep, philosophical questions were too mentally exhausting. So I had to take a break... from whatever I was doing at that point, I don't remember anymore. What was it? How did I get to this subject?

Ok, it doesn't matter. The point is that I'm NOT a procrastinator, ok? I have multiple interests that don't fit traditional schooling system, that's totally different. You know what? I should start a YouTube channel about that. About how society tries to measure our success according to outdated standards... A motivational channel telling people to take life by the reins and live life on their own terms... And since I'm not a procrastinator I'm gonna start right now and-

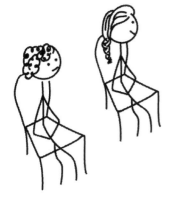

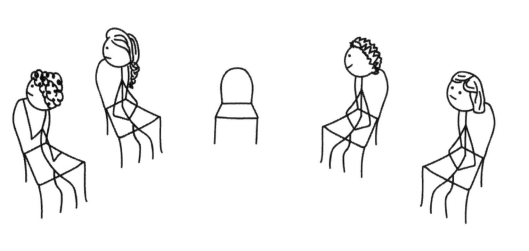

Now, having seen that I have explored all these angles and that I'm fully conscious of all these ways procrastination can manifest, you must be asking: "So Cristina, did you get any better at beating procrastination?

No! Obviously.

I still suck so much at deadlines, I leave everything to such a last minute, that on my first festival, the Adelaide Fringe, in Australia, I actually managed... to miss the deadline to register my show. I was ONE HOUR late.

This went beyond just procrastinating: the registration deadline was 4th of October at 5 pm... and my brain had computed "5th of October at 4 pm". So you can imagine my panic when I logged into the registration page on the 4th in the morning, happily thinking that I still had a whole day ahead to finalise it, and read "Registrations closed, see you next year".

No!! It couldn't be!! THIS was the year! I had made plans, I had built hopes! I had finally taken action!

Spoiler alert, I made it in spite of it. I called the lovely organisers. I was prepared to beg, to give long explanations, huge justifications, to expand on heartfelt apologies... But they simply said, "No problem mate, you're in"!

And this is why... I love Australia. Their world-famous laidback lifestyle is perfect for my messy ways - just imagine: had this been the "Germany Fringe"... it wouldn't have happened. Not a chance.

But I couldn't just simply call as soon as I saw I was locked out. Because it was the 4th of October in the morning for me, in Europe... but it was 6 pm in Australia. No one was left in the office, business hours were till 5. So I actually had to wait 15 hours until it was 9 am in Australia, and someone was in the office to pick up the phone. 15 desperate hours of crying, screaming, having panic attacks, inappropriately messaging a lot of people I didn't know, asking for help (yep, it wasn't cute)... I even resorted to praying. And I'm yet to meet an atheist who's never resorted to praying in a moment of ultimate desperation. I'm not an atheist though, I'm agnostic, I don't really know what's out there, up there, down there, midichlorians in our blood (seriously George Lucas, why do you have to ruin it for us?)... But I'm pretty sure that if Catholic God exists, he's just getting to the point where he'll look at his Galaxy - you know, "Galaxy", a phone fit for a god... (cue to drum rimshot - I'm here every Tuesday, try the fish) - see that it's me calling, and say "Eh. Rebound".

I did make the Fringe, though, and you may say God helped me... but as I said, I don't necessarily believe in God... I believe in science. Science is what comes to my rescue in my direst procrastinator hours...

On today's episode: You've all probably heard of the Relativity Theory, devised by Einstein. And you probably heard of the Quantum Theory devised by... some other dudes. Both are solid, elegant theories that explain how the universe works. But not together. Together they clash. They clash like your aunt Amelia's desire to keep a diet and the spoonfuls of Nutella that she keeps shoving into her mouth.

How is that possible? Well... some scientists finally worked out a scenario where both theories work together seamlessly. Like you and your BFF trying to decode your ex's posts on social media.

Both theories only make sense together if... this universe is a hologram. And this opens the doors to all sorts of fascinating new discussions:

Are we just a projection? Who's projecting? And are we the ONLY projection? Do we... live in a simulation?

Is there a richer, more successful version of us living in a parallel universe, in a different timeline? And what if there's already a more successful version of us in another timeline? Does that mean that every effort that we make in this timeline is useless, as this is not the timeline where we're supposed to be?

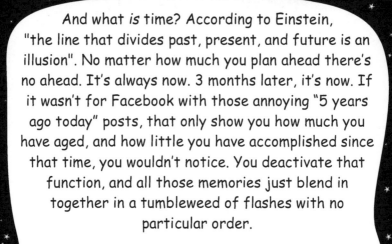

And what *is* time? According to Einstein, "the line that divides past, present, and future is an illusion". No matter how much you plan ahead there's no ahead. It's always now. 3 months later, it's now. If it wasn't for Facebook with those annoying "5 years ago today" posts, that only show you how much you have aged, and how little you have accomplished since that time, you wouldn't notice. You deactivate that function, and all those memories just blend in together in a tumbleweed of flashes with no particular order.

And speaking of getting old, don't miss on the next episode how with the advances of technology, biotechnology, nanotechnology, age medicine, CRISPR editing, transhumanism... we'll finally be able to conquer human ageing.

Good night.

Wow... THAT'S IT!!! Time is an illusion!!! Which means... I have all the time in the world!!! I'll never get old...!!! I'll never age...!!! I'll never die!!! I'm gonna live FOREVER!!!

You're realising now this is no TED Talk where I "analyse procrastination" and "offer a fresh perspective" on how to solve procrastination. Sorry, I have no solution for your problems. #NoRefunds.

But I had to end the show. And I didn't want to end with a moral lesson, because who am I to give advice? So I first thought about an ending for the show where I'd say "let's just hope that these science advances happen during our lifetime, and that our time can be extended, and our age can be reversed before it's too late, otherwise we're pretty fucked!"

I thought about ending the show by initially getting an usher to ask you to write what YOU have been procrastinating on on a little piece of paper, and then put it in The Big Bag of Postponed Dreams-

*not just a Tesco bag that I got last minute because I didn't have time to prepare a proper bag - that was totally on purpose.

- and then draw from it and read some, raising awareness that we need to start acting on the things that matter right now.

Oooh, see? That WAS on purpose!

I thought about ending the show with a powerful bold punchline like: "The ultimate deadline... is your life!" (life - life - life -life) ← *that's the echo.*

But look at me! I didn't even have to come up with an ending for the show, and I ended up speaking for 50 minutes, yeah? As promised! I've pulled it off in the end, didn't I? Like always! I did it!

I believe I'll always pull it off in the end! I believe my time will always be magically extended! I believe that as long as I keep being immature and dating guys half my age (which is totally legal, because I'm 36), I'm not gonna get one wrinkle, one grey hair! I'll always be young, fresh, promising! I believe I'll always pull it off in the end! I believe in science! I believe in god! I believe in miracles! I did it, guys! I did it! Woo-hoo!

***

This was my show. As you can see, I did write a final product in the end, mostly in time (I have to confess I came up with this ending on the plane to Australia, on the eve of the opening night). But although I didn't want to have an ending with a "moral" (you know... "Kids, eat your greens!") - first, because that was a comedy, second because I have no qualification as a psychologist, psychiatrist, or scientist of any kind, and third because, as I said, who am I to give advice on this matter?, so I didn't want to come across as lecturing people - I did end up coming up with a very interesting thought:

When we procrastinate on artistic or entrepreneurial projects, or any venture that we've never done before, maybe we are experiencing one of the 4 Stages of Escape. They're 4 stages of clarity on what step to take next, really, but the name is fancy because of the imaginary (and a bit supernatural) scenario that illustrates it:

Imagine one day you wake up in a cube-shaped room.

There are no windows, there are no doors, but there are a lot of screens on the walls, like high definition coloured CCTV scenes of the world outside. You can see the world out there, so you know that it exists. You even see that there are other people in other cubes. It only seems impossible for <u>you</u> to be out, because you are inside this seemingly hermetic cube.

Now imagine some time passes, and one day, in one of these screens, you watch someone you know managing to escape their cube. You don't see how this person does it, but you had seen they were in a cube before, and now they're out. The question that immediately crosses your mind is: if they did it, how can I do it too? It suddenly feels less impossible for you to eventually get out. Your hopes are enticed. And you start looking for an exit. You start looking for cues in the screens, you start looking around to see if there's any lever, any secret passage...

And after some time, you eventually do find a little hatch, that takes you to a tunnel. The tunnel takes you to a massive labyrinth. Now, of course you can venture by yourself into the labyrinth (or maybe you feel overwhelmed and just sit down, feeling that just going into the labyrinth is too scary - that's also an option). There's only one detail: the labyrinth is totally dark. Whatever you choose consumes a lot of time, and doesn't advance you much.

One day, either at the entrance, if you decided to stay, or at some point in a dead corner of the labyrinth, if you decided to enter, you stumble upon... a friend of yours! Someone you know. Someone different than the person you saw escaping, that one is out already. This friend of yours has a torch. And a map. And invites you to join their escape journey. They can't get you out, this is something that you have to do by yourself, but you can follow them and assist them with their escape, like they did - they assisted someone else with their escape before. This will be great experience for you, great training, you're not going to be just two lost people walking around randomly, guided by nothing but hope and a strong will to leave.

You go through the maze with them, sometimes even taking notes of mistakes, rough paths, and turns that lead to dead ends. You both reach the exit door. And off they go. They leave. You're not allowed to, you are magically returned to the initial point.

But now you know how to leave, now you're even aware of different paths that you could use, that would make it easier to get out faster, paths that are more efficient, less slimy... it's still going to be a bit of a scary adventure, but you make it, and you get out, to enjoy the world.

There were four stages in this escape.

1) The Cube

When you are in the Cube Stage, achieving something seems out of your reality. You see other people doing it, but it seems so far-fetched to you, that you don't even rank it as a priority, as much as you daydream about it. You trick yourself into thinking "I'll do it one day", but this day will never come, because you'll never feel ready, you feel that something's missing to "ignite your process". There's a long list of other unrealistic things that ideally need to happen first so you can do the other, then the other, then the other, until you finally feel "ready" to take the actual action that is going to begin this particular project.

2) The Screen

When you're on the Screen Stage, that is, when you see someone you know doing what you're dreaming of doing - even if you don't know how they made it - you immediately think that this is more possible to you, even if you still don't know how. It needs to be someone you know, not just "someone". Random people on Instagram or TV belong to the realm of far-fetched. It doesn't have to be a close friend. It can be an ex, a coworker, a friend's friend. In my case, it even happened with someone who had done the same one-day course as me a couple of years before: she had been there, in the same course as me, in the same "position" as me, and suddenly I heard that she was writing, performing and selling shows. I've heard of people quitting their job to start their business or to travel the world after they saw a coworker doing it. It takes one person in your inner circle, your social circle, professional circle, or in your circle of reference to do it before you: a fire ignites. It doesn't seem much, but there's a huge leap from thinking "that's not for me" to thinking "if So-And-So did it, how can I do it too"?

3) The Labyrinth

When you're in the Labyrinth Stage, you're really trying to make it happen, but you're tangled. You're spinning the hamster wheel. You firmly believe that you can do it, which is a win already, but if in the Screen Stage you didn't even know how to start, here what makes you stuck is the maze of information, procedures, steps, directions you've been taking, even advice. There's so much advice out there, that it may be overwhelming, not to mention contradictory, or worse, ill, unfitting, opposed to your ethics: say the advice someone gives you to get clients for your business is to add every random person you can find on LinkedIn and Facebook and spam them with your offer, and being against that, you go back to thinking "this is not for me" ("if that's what it takes") and go back to stuck mode. The problem with trying to DYI your way in the dark is that, more often than not, we may remain lost in the maze for years on end.

4) The Hike

When you're in the Hike Stage, you're finally convinced that what you want to do is possible and very realistic to you, and you finally see some light and direction, but you're not the one holding the light or the map. It doesn't matter, because you're now so close: not only you are already working on what you want to work, even if in a smaller or coadjuvant capacity, gaining hands-on experience, but you may also experience incredible insights. And that's because very, VERY seldom in life, people invent things out of thin air. Most inventions are an evolution of something that already existed, and all of them happen because the creator finally saw what was not working with the old system, why it's not working, and how it could work.

On the same note, it's not uncommon that only by closely following, observing, working with someone who's considered a bigger authority or more experienced, we develop the most kindling feeling of all: the moment when we think "wait a minute, I can do better than them". In a very conscious, inspired, clarity-driven way. It's not about being spiteful, or delusional, it's not like looking at a modern painting you don't understand and saying, "my five-year-old could paint better". It's really about having this urge of knowing how to improve something that you see isn't being done the best possible way, having this spark of a new idea. Maybe you are going to be better than them, maybe you are simply going to be just as good, but different, and this is when you have found your voice. This is the ultimate signal that you are ready. It's very hard to procrastinate when you're on the end of your Hike Stage.

Of course sometimes we procrastinate on de-cluttering our closet or doing our taxes. But this is something that only takes a little bit of inspiration, or of course, has a deadline. But if you want to create something that is innovative, and it's scary for you because you've never done before, and you've been procrastinating for years, chances are you are in one of these stages.

It's not a procrastination that lacks disposition, it's a procrastination that lacks the vision that this project is possible for you, or the direction that will remove the frustration of eternal and dead-end trial-and-error, or the spark that will finally take you from follower to leader, from observer to creator. This knowledge is one of the main contributors of springing you into action, and the lack thereof is one of the main factors that can hold you back from taking action.

So instead of beating yourself up by saying "I'm procrastinating", your task here, your next step, should be trying to identify where in the Escape you are:

1) Find someone similar to you who's doing what you're trying to do. Actively search for any sort of example or reference that can motivate you and show you this sense of possibility. My favourite quote from the movie Patch Adams happens when he moves into the student dorm, and his new roommate says "I don't mean to be rude, but aren't you a little old to be starting medical school?", and he answers "You know, Babe Ruth was 39 when he joined the Yankees." The roommate says "No, he wasn't", to what Patch says "You're right. But I could really use an example like that".

2) Find out how they did it, or better yet, try to find someone else who is doing it or who has recently done it - because the ones you heard "made it" are, more often than not, not the people who are going to have coffee with you to tell you how they made it.

3) Find someone you can collaborate with, who's more advanced in the process than you. Rather than trying to reinvent the wheel from your room, having a mentor can do wonders to fast-track your process in the project you are trying to create.

4) And of course, trust your inner voice when it says "wait a minute, you can do it better than them!" This voice is YOUR voice, and that's the true hallmark of a successful creator. You're ready.

May you have a fulfilled and productive life. Happy achieving!

It's the Fringe

CAUTION: Deadline Ahead

Cristina Lark

up and I... put three mi-nutes in the bag! It's only been one minute, yeah?

This is gonna be harder than I thought. Ok, ok, let me see...

It's the Fringe What the fuck I'm do-ing with my life...? Nah, this is

horrible. I'll finish writing this one later... at some point... in the future...

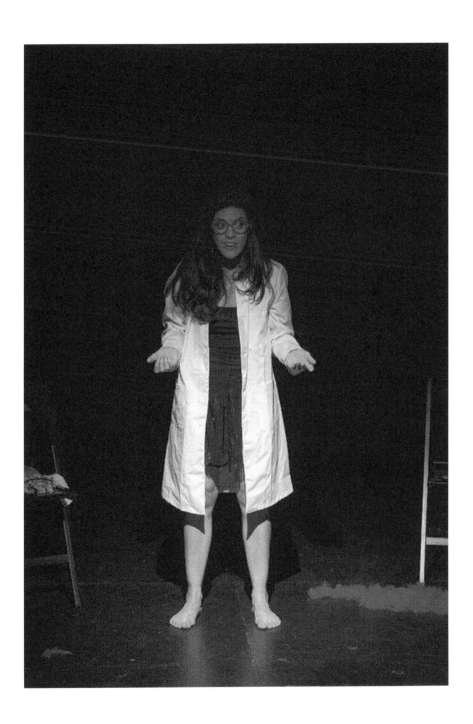

Photos by Emma Nan Hu. London, October 2018.
All Rights Reserved.

Tour reviews:

"Will resonate on a level you would never believe. Lark is absolutely stone-cold hilarious. She is a clever comedian at the top of her game. If nods of affirmation were applause, Lark would receive a standing ovation after every statement!"
- *The Fourth Wall, Perth, 2019*

"Hilarious narrative. Relatable, boisterous and quick-witted. Brilliantly delivered."
- *Weekend Notes, Adelaide, 2019*

"Spot-on observations. Very sharp and honest. Held a mirror up to the audience. A funny and sharp look into the world of procrastination."
- *Upside News, Adelaide, 2019*

"A high-energy meta show, which takes audiences on a crash course through the life of a procrastinator".
– *FringeFeed, Perth, 2019*

"The audience has no choice but to bow down before it's new Jedi Master. Lark's a ball of fire. Guaranteed to make you feel better about yourself"
- *The Advertiser, Adelaide, 2018*

"It's hard not to love Cristina Lark. She's a talented comedienne. A delightful speaker and a great actress"
- *EdFringeReview, Edinburgh, 2018*

"Cristina Lark is a firecracker with a mind that moves as fast as lightning" - *Arthur's Seat, Edinburgh, 2018*

"Cristina Lark is more than a comedy firecracker onstage: try a full-blown fireworks display. Talented and very funny. A hilarious hour that was over all too quickly".
- *Chuck Moore Reviews, Adelaide, 2018*

ABOUT THE AUTHOR

Actor, public speaking coach and world-class procrastinator, Cristina Lark lived and performed in the UK, Australia, Spain and Brazil.

With an MA at renowned RADA but impossible to cast in any stereotypical roles due to her weird accent, she writes her own material, like the webseries about dating disasters "It's Not You...", reviewed "go back to your country, sweetheart" by Brexiteers, but nominated for "Best Comedy Ensemble" at Rio Web Fest.

She works in English, Portuguese, Spanish, Catalan, French and Italian. She also writes, directs, devises, casts and produces for stage and screen.

Reading back, it's amazing how much she's accomplished, given her long history of procrastination and leaving everything until the last minute.

Instagram: @cristinalark

42682825R00074

Printed in Poland
by Amazon Fulfillment
Poland Sp. z o.o., Wrocław